CONTENTS

KT-432-164

CHAPTER 1

SCHOOL BLUES

I sit in the lesson and watch the girls around me. They all have perfectly styled hair. Their bags all have cool brand-name labels. I glance at my own beaten up messenger bag and try to focus on whatever our teacher, Ms DiSousa, is saying.

"Nice hair, Grace," Ella Hayes hisses from behind me.

I seriously doubt her words are meant as a compliment. Last year, as Ella was leaving the hairdressers, she spotted me leaving the charity shop across the street. She's made fun of my hair and clothes ever since.

Unlike Ella's perfectly straight, shiny red hair, my curly blonde hair can be frizzy. My mum works really hard, but I know we don't have the money for me to go to a posh hairdressers or buy expensive hair products. I usually wear a headband to keep my hair tidy.

For my competitive tap dance team, I just twist it into a bun. It's not the most glamorous look, but at Ms Marianne's Academy of Dance, *everyone's* hair is messy after two hours of sweating.

I suppose I should be grateful Ella's never seen me like that. And at least she mocks me out of earshot of everyone else at school.

I glance at the clock. Ten minutes until I can leave for dance class. Dance is the only good thing about Wednesdays.

Ms DiSousa turns back to the board, and Ella kicks my chair. "Sorry," she says.

I doubt it was an accident. But knowing Ella, she'd insist it was if I tried to bring it up to a teacher. Not that I haven't thought about doing that. But it's not worth it. It would just make things worse.

I sigh under my breath and try to focus on Ms Marianne's. The dance school is my happy place. None of the other dancers go to the same school as me. None of them know I don't quite fit in here. At Ms Marianne's, no one cares that my leotards are a bit faded or a bit too big. The girls on my dance team only care that I can move my tap shoes like lightning.

I put my homework in my folder and get ready to bolt. Three. Two. One. *Riiing!* I zoom out of the door.

* * *

From the outside, Ms Marianne's Academy of Dance is just a tiny brick building. The inside is another story. Studios line the corridor. When it's sunny, the rooms are bright with natural light. At night, overhead ceiling lights brighten the rooms.

I walk to the office first to say hello to the receptionist – also known as my mum. I love having her here. The truth is, I'm here because of her. We're only able to afford lessons at Ms Marianne's because of extra office work Mum does in exchange for my dance tuition and costumes.

"How was school, honey?" Mum asks. She brushes her curly blonde hair from her eyes.

I shrug and force a smile. "Same as ever. Happy to be here."

I haven't told my mum about Ella. She doesn't need the stress.

It's just the two of us, and I know she's tired enough with all the hours she works. I help when I can by taking care of stuff around the house or taking the bus to and from Ms Marianne's instead of making Mum leave work to drive me.

She hugs me. "I'm happy you're here too."

"Have you seen Jada, Gabby or Brie?" I ask, looking around for my closest friends on the dance team.

Mum laughs. "They were in here ten minutes ago asking about you."

I smile properly now. I love tap dance, which I have on Monday, Thursday and Saturday afternoons, but Wednesdays are even better. That's when I have all-team ballet.

No matter their dance speciality, all the dancers at Ms Marianne's are required to take ballet. It strengthens our muscles and helps with flexibility.

Ballet is harder for me than tap, but as Jada, Gabby, Brie and I all specialize in different dances, it's the only time we have a class together.

And lately, with school being less fun than ever, seeing my best friends is everything.

CHAPTER 2

BALLET PRACTICE

I rest my left leg on the ballet barre, move my chest to my knee, and cradle my toes in my hands. It is a deep stretch and feels good after a long day at school. The truth is, every day is a long day at school.

At Ms Marianne's, all my worries seem to float away. Here, it's just me and the dance floor.

I place my left leg on the floor and move my right foot to the barre, repeating the stretch.

"Hey, you," Jada says, walking into the studio. She's wearing a turquoise leotard and ballet slippers, her usual dance clothes as ballet is her speciality. "How are you?"

"Always better once I'm here," I say, grinning.

Jada only moved here a few months ago, but we've become very close. Still, as close as I am to Jada and my other friends here, no one knows about Ella. I totally trust them, but I don't want to bring all that negative energy into my happy place.

"I hear you," says Jada. Her heels touch, and she bends her knees as she lowers herself into a *plié.*

"Brie and Gabby have arrived!" Gabby half-shouts, half-sings as she and Brie walk into the room. Brie blushes. Even though she always looks fierce and confident during her hip-hop routines, she hates to be the centre of attention.

They join us at the barre and begin moving their feet into the five ballet positions as the rest of the dancers filter in.

Ms Marianne arrives at exactly four o'clock.

The school has different teachers for the other dance specialities, but Ms Marianne teaches all the ballet classes herself. "Good afternoon, ladies," she says. "We will begin with our feet positions."

We line up with partners. As usual, Gabby and Brie work together; Jada and I do the same. I can hear Gabby talking about her *abuela* wanting her to learn how to cook. Brie chats about a holiday her dads are planning.

I move to sixth position, my feet parallel to each other, and practise stepping out to the side and forward. It's a basic step but something I need to practise. Keeping feet parallel is important in most tap moves and jumps, and it's something I forget to do when focusing on a new step.

Next to me, Jada practises fifth position. It's a harder move, but she easily touches the toes of one foot to her opposite heel.

I work on my knees next, bending them until

my heels lift off the ground. This helps me remember to bend my knees in tap. Dropping a heel with bent knees is easier than with straight legs.

"When are you finally going to take up ballet?" Jada teases.

Some girls specialize in more than one dance, but tap is enough for me. "And upstage you?" I tease back. "I'll let you shine."

Jada laughs.

I raise myself up on my toes to strengthen my calves and heels, then lower back down. The concentration necessary for ballet bores me, but I'm thankful for it when tap class comes around. Ballet helps me have better balance in tap.

"Water break," calls Ms Marianne.

Brie, Gabby, Jada and I grab our water bottles and huddle together.

"Is it just me," asks Brie, "or does this class

seem especially long today?"

"It's not just you," says Gabby. "I want my jazz shoes!"

Jada pouts. "You all say the same thing every week."

I throw my arm around Jada. "Maybe we can convince Ms Marianne to make each of our dance styles a requirement too." I wink.

Jada chokes on her water. "No thanks. Ballet is more my speed. Concentrating on this helps take my mind off everything else."

I nod. "When I'm here, nothing else matters."

CHAPTER 3

BAD SURPRISE

The next day after school, I run to catch the bus. I get off just before Ms Marianne's and right in front of Sunny's Second-hand Shop. Mum and I have been shopping here for years. It's a great place to get dance stuff. Brand-new stuff can be really expensive.

I've been saving for new tap shoes. Sunny called yesterday to say someone had brought in a pair in my size. Talk about good luck!

"Just the lady I've been waiting for," Sunny says when I walk in. Her wide smile matches her name and the cheery, bright-yellow walls of her shop. She reaches under the counter and pulls out a pair of tap shoes.

I quickly examine them. The heel and toe plates look barely worn. I try on the shiny black shoes and jump around on the floor. My heart soars when I hear the clear *click-clack* they make.

"Thank you!" I say.

"My pleasure, hon," Sunny says with a smile. "You know how much I love you guys."

I pay for the shoes and place them carefully in my dance bag before changing into my trainers. Excited, I walk out of Sunny's shop. I can't wait to use them in today's class.

* * *

When I get to Ms Marianne's, I quickly change into my leotard, put on my new tap shoes, and put my bag in a locker. Then I head to the front office.

"Look at these," I say to my mum. I do a little dance to show off my new shoes.

"Looking good," she says, grinning.

Not wanting to be late, I hurry down the hall to my studio. Most of the girls are already there doing warm-ups at the barre, talking, or tapping on the floor. Tap class always has a livelier vibe than ballet. The moves here are freer and quicker.

"Hi, ladies!" Ms Anne, our teacher, calls as she enters the room. She flashes a bright smile.

"I have an announcement," she continues. "A new student will be joining us today. Her dance school closed a month ago. She auditioned for our team last weekend. She's just getting changed and will be here shortly."

I wonder how old the new girl is and what she's like. I was new last year, so I know how hard it can be. I make a mental note to introduce her to Gabby, Brie and Jada.

As we wait, I stand on my left foot and brush my right foot forward and back across the floor. *Scuffle, scuffle.* I repeat the move. My right toe hits the floor behind me. *Toe, toe.*

I pause and take a sip of water as I see Ms Anne wave someone in from the corridor.

"Class," says Ms Anne, "please welcome our new student . . ." She taps her hands on her knees like a drum roll.

A loud rushing noise fills my ears. Despite the water, my mouth goes dry. My hands shake, and I wrap them tightly around my water bottle. I know what she's going to say. I knew the second I saw the red hair.

"Ella Hayes," Ms Anne finishes.

CHAPTER 4

No more Happy place

I keep my eyes closed for another second because I know as soon as I open them, I'll see Ella's green eyes glaring at me. Then Ms Anne claps her hands, and my eyes spring open. I make sure I look anywhere but at Ella.

"Let's begin our combination," says Ms Anne.

"Ms Anne," Ella says in a sweet voice I've never heard before, "I know Grace. Can I stand next to her?"

Ms Anne's face lights up. "Of course! Just make sure you stay focused."

She winks at me, but I can't smile. I slowly put down my water bottle and try to focus on the combination.

"Now I'll get to see you all the time," Ella whispers in my ear when she gets to her place.

"Lucky me," I mutter.

Ms Anne starts the music, and my legs move in their memorized routine. *Scuffle, scuffle, toe, toe.* I follow with two ball-heel combinations, alternating touching the balls and heels of my feet to the floor.

Ella's feet get too close to mine, and I quickly jump back, afraid she'll step on my toes. She sniggers.

Get out of my head! I think. *Focus!*

My favourite step, a wing, is next. I feel Ella next to me, watching. My feet move to the side, and the balls of my feet brush against the floor. My arms circle wide.

Jada always flaps her arms like a bird when I do this move. I smile thinking about it. The funny image calms me and makes it easier to ignore Ella.

I rock back on my heels for a heel stand and hold the position. It's not easy to balance, so I'm proud of myself for holding the move.

"Not bad," hisses Ella. I lose my concentration and stumble.

"Keep going, Grace," calls Ms Anne. "You can do this!"

Except I can't. Not today. And if Ella is a permanent addition to my dance team, I don't know if I'll be able to *do it* ever again.

* * *

That night, I push the pasta around on my plate and hope my mum doesn't notice. Of course, she does.

"What's up?" Mum asks.

"Difficult practice," I say. I force myself to eat a few strands of spaghetti.

"Even with your fantastic new shoes?" she asks, smiling.

I want to cry thinking about how excited I was about the shoes. That feels like a lifetime ago compared to how awful I feel now. I nod, afraid if I speak I'll start bawling.

"I've seen you master loads of moves in a short time." Mum squeezes my hand. "I have faith in you."

"Thanks," I whisper. I used to have faith in myself too. I need to get that back. I need to get my mind focused back on my feet and off Ella Hayes.

I eat a bit more pasta for fuel and go to the spare room to practise. *You can do this,* I tell myself.

Scuffle, scuffle, toe, toe. My feet move quickly, and I smile at the happy *click-clack* sound. Next I shift to the ball-heel combos and wings. I wave my arms extra wide and add more energy. I end with a heel stand and hold the move for a count of ten.

Yes! I cheer silently. I close my eyes to savour the moment.

Suddenly Ella's face looms behind my eyelids. I open my eyes and sigh heavily. I know I can't let her ruin my happy place, but I don't know how to stop her.

CHAPTER 5

FROM BAD TO WORSE

At school the next day, I doodle pictures of tap shoes in my notebook while I wait for Ms DiSousa to begin.

"Fun class yesterday, wasn't it?" says Ella, nudging my shoulder.

I don't look at her. "Yep."

"It looked like you had some trouble with the heel stand," Ella continues, sounding less than sincere. "That's a shame."

I suck in air through my teeth and press my pen hard against the paper.

She smirks. "I wouldn't want to talk about it either."

"What made you choose Ms Marianne's anyway?" I ask. I need to know.

"It wasn't my first choice, but my mum likes how close it is. That school is lucky to have me. *I* don't fumble *my* heel stands." She laughs and takes her seat before I can respond.

Ms DiSousa starts talking about the clothing styles of the 1700s, and I look around the classroom. The girl in front of me, Olivia, is wearing jeans with a designer label on the back. Next to me, another classmate, Maddie, taps her manicured nails on her desk and absently plays with the charm on her gold bracelet.

I do my best with clothes, but my stuff isn't nearly as nice as what the other girls wear. Today, I'm wearing one of my favourite outfits: a soft pink jumper, jeggings and shoes with chunky heels.

It's all from Sunny's. Sunny even found a necklace with a pink heart charm that goes perfectly with the jumper but, as I look around, I feel out of place.

When the bell rings, Ella takes her time gathering her books. My heart beats quickly because I know she's waiting for me.

"I'll see you tomorrow," Ella says when we're at the door.

"Right," I mumble.

"By the way, that jumper is one of your better finds. You almost can't tell it wasn't good enough for anyone else." She laughs and pushes past me as tears sting my eyes.

* * *

On Saturday, I hang around in the corridor with Brie, Jada and Gabby. We're all waiting for our dance classes to start.

They haven't met Ella yet – she started after Wednesday's all-team class – and I haven't told them about her. But when I see Ella leaving the changing room, I know that's about to change.

"Hi, Grace," Ella says when she spots us.

My palms get sweaty. I can't pretend I didn't hear her with my friends watching. I slowly wave hello.

She comes over. "I'm Ella," she introduces herself. "I just joined the tap dance team." Her smile hides how mean she is.

"You dance with Grace?" asks Jada. She looks from me to Ella.

"Uh-huh. We go to the same school too!"

Gabby, Brie and Jada stare at me. They must be wondering why I haven't mentioned her before.

"Classes, everyone!" calls Ms Marianne.

I wave goodbye to my friends, and Jada mouths, "We'll talk later."

I desperately *don't* want to talk about it later. I already know it won't do any good. Ella never does anything when she knows other people are watching. But at the same time, I know I'll need my friends at my side if I'm going to get through this.

I focus on my warm-up and ignore Ella's attempts to distract me. *Ball, ball.* The balls of my feet tap the floor. *Heel, heel.* My heels beat a rhythm. *Toe, Toe.*

The sound of the plates against hardwood calms me, and I quicken my pace, repeating the whole combination. I add a quick ball change. I place my right foot behind me and rock on the ball of it while my left foot is off the ground. I repeat the same movement with the left foot behind me. Hearing my shoes *clacking* with each move reminds me why this is my happy place.

"Bravo, Grace!" Ms Anne shouts above the music. "That's some fancy footwork!"

I grin and hear Ella grunt beside me. Her feet aren't moving as quickly as mine. My ankles are loose and ready as I wait for Ms Anne to give us more instructions.

"Today we're adding a new move to our combination," our teacher says. "Two buffalos and two shuffles. Watch me."

Ms Anne jumps on her right leg to start the buffalo. Then she brushes the floor twice with the ball of her left foot. *Click!* She jumps on the floor with her left foot and brings the right one up to cross at her left knee. She repeats the buffalo.

"And now the shuffles," she says. She brushes the ball of her right foot across the hardwood floor, then repeats the move with her left. "Put it all together!"

She completes two buffalos, followed by two shuffles. The room erupts with *clickety-clacks* as we all do the same.

"Excellent work, ladies!" says Ms Anne. "Well done, Grace!"

"Well done, Grace," Ella mimics under her breath.

I feel my stomach tightening and try to push away the sick feeling. *You can do this.*

"From the top!" Ms Anne calls, turning to face the other side of the room.

We begin the combination from the very beginning. *Scuffle, scuffle, toe, toe. Wing.* My feet move to the side, and my arms circle wide. I lean back on my heels for the heel stand.

Ella shifts closer, and I start the buffalo before she can knock me down. I jump on my right foot, then brush the floor twice with the toe of my left foot.

My heels stay off the ground, just as Ms Anne had demonstrated minutes before. I repeat the move, then move my toes forward and back across the floor for the shuffles.

Suddenly Ella bumps me – hard. I fall to the floor, and my face reddens. Ms Anne turns around to see what happened.

"So sorry!" Ella exclaims. I can tell by her satisfied expression that she doesn't mean it. But Ms Anne can only hear Ella's voice. She can't see her face.

"No, you're not!" I hiss back.

Ella shrugs. "Not all of us can be as good as you." She glares at my tap shoes. "Maybe whoever threw those away sprinkled them with magic fairy dust first."

I pick myself up and turn away from Ella. Seconds ago, I was so proud of myself. How does Ella manage to steal my confidence every time?

CHAPTER 6

CONFESSIONS

After practice, Brie, Jada, Gabby and I sit on the soft blue carpet of Jada's bedroom. They all wanted the details about Ella. I've just finished telling them about the latest incident.

"But wait," says Jada. "I still don't get why she picks on you."

I stare at my hands. I haven't told them about the charity shop run-in or how I don't fit in with the girls at my school.

"C'mon," says Gabby, gently bumping me with her shoulder, "you can tell us anything."

I bite my lip. They like me. They're my friends. "She saw me coming out of a charity shop once," I say quietly.

No one says anything.

"So . . . what?" Brie finally asks.

"So," I say, "she knows I shop there. No one at my school would be caught dead there. All the other girls at my school get their hair and nails done, they all have new clothes, you know . . ." My voice trails off.

Gabby throws her hands up in the air. "Are you serious? I get hand-me-downs from my cousins all the time. Who cares?"

How come they don't see this as a big deal? Maybe they don't get it.

"My tap shoes are from Sunny's Second-hand Shop," I say quietly. "Most of my stuff is. We can't really afford new stuff." I raise my head to look at them.

"This is ridiculous!" cries Jada. "Who cares where you get your clothes or how much money your family has?"

"Exactly!" says Brie. "That's just crazy. Someone at my school once said something rude about me having two dads. People can be so stupid – and mean."

"This isn't OK," says Gabby, slamming her fist on the carpet. "We love you, Grace. And I love your tap shoes."

"And I love your hair," says Jada.

"And I love your face," Brie adds, laughing.

I laugh too. "Thanks, guys. I just . . . I don't know how to stop her from getting to me."

"We won't let her," Gabby says firmly.

"Agreed," Brie says. "You are too good a dancer to let her put you off."

CHAPTER 7

OFFBEAT

For the rest of the weekend I think about what my friends said. It felt good to finally tell them and to know they're on my side. I replay what Brie said too: "You are too good a dancer to let her put you off."

On Monday, I avoid Ella at school. I have my books ready so I can walk into the lesson just as it's about to begin and zoom out the second it finishes.

When I get to Ms Marianne's after school, my head is clearer than it's been all week. I change into a black leotard and my tap shoes and look at myself in the mirror.

You can do this, I tell myself. I take a deep breath. Then I hear Ella's voice in the corridor, and my palms get sweaty. *Shake it off. Don't let her in your head.*

But I can't seem to do it. Everything looks wrong. My leotard looks more faded than it did seconds ago. I notice pieces of hair sticking out from my bun. Even scuff marks I'd barely noticed on my tap shoes now seem to flash at me like hazard lights. I grab my water and run out of the changing room before Ella arrives.

I think about asking Ms Anne for a new part in the routine, but I don't know what reason I would give. I hate that the place I love has turned into a prison.

I try to focus on the shiny floor, the barre, the large mirrors and the giant window. I practise basic tap moves, *toe and heel, toe and heel*, just to get the *cloppity-clop* sounds in my head.

Before my mum started working here last year, I would watch internet videos of tap dancers non-stop and practise moves on our kitchen floor. Sometimes I went to free dance workshops at the community centre.

I've come a long way since then, I remind myself. *I'm on the dance team! Why am I letting Ella take all that away from me?*

I practise the combination in front of the mirror and feel calmer. I tune out the voices around me and focus on the *click-clack-clop* of my tap shoes. My feet brush against the floor faster and faster.

Then, out of nowhere, someone shoves me hard from behind. I stumble.

"You should really pay attention to where you're practising," says Ella slyly.

Furious, I whip around. I've tried ignoring Ella at school, but that hasn't worked.

My mouth is dry, but I swallow and find my voice. "What is your problem?" I ask.

The words don't come out strong like I'd imagined in my head. My voice is weak and shaky.

Ella laughs and shakes her head. She pulls at my leotard. "You really need to find clothes that fit."

I know my friends are right about clothes and money not mattering, but my mum has been working so hard to get me here. I feel tears forming in my eyes and can't stop them.

Ella looks satisfied and makes her way over to another section of the barre. Seeing me break down is what she's been wanting, but I can't let her win.

"And a one and a two," Ms Anne's clear voice calls.

When did she come in? I wonder.

My head feels like it's underwater. I try to move my feet – *scuffle, scuffle* – but I'm a second behind everyone else. I tap my toe on the floor, but everyone is a beat ahead. I can't get the rhythm back.

"Having problems?" Ella whispers, just loud enough for me to hear.

Tears slip out of my eyes. I can't take any more. I grab my water and run out of the studio.

CHAPTER 8

GETTING BACK THE GROOVE

"You're awfully quiet," Mum says that evening. We're watching our favourite programme, *Dance Stars*. I can hardly focus on it.

I shrug. "Tired."

"You didn't wait for me to give you a lift home after your class today," she says softly.

I feel the tears coming again and turn away.

Mum strokes my hair. "Is dance getting too hard? Is it interfering with school?" she asks.

I almost laugh. *No,* school *is interfering with* dance, I want to tell her. Instead I say, "It's none of those things."

I look at Mum's concerned face. We tell each other everything. I *want* to tell her about Ella. But what would she do about Ella anyway? What would happen in tap class, at my locker, at school? The problem isn't just at tap. It's everywhere. I need to stop being afraid so I can get her out of my head for good.

"I'm here for you if you want to talk," Mum tells me. Worry lines pucker around her mouth and eyes.

"I know," I say. My friends are here for me too. Now it's up to me to make a change.

* * *

On Wednesday, Ms Marianne lets me come in early to practise before ballet. After Monday, I need to pull myself together.

"I thought I heard someone in here," says Ms Anne, walking into the studio. "How are you?"

I blush. I hadn't explained just running out of the studio the other day. "I'm OK. I was having a bad day on Monday. I'm sorry."

Ms Anne cocks her head to the side. "We've all been there." She smiles. "Do you want to show me the combination now? I have time."

"Yes, please!" I beam.

I shake out my wrists and ankles and take a deep breath. Ms Anne turns on the music. My right foot brushes forward and back across the hardwood floor. *Scuffle, scuffle.* I repeat the move with my left, then tap my toes. *Toe, toe.*

The familiar sounds fill my body, and I relax. The ball-heel combinations are next, and my feet quickly tap the floor, not missing a beat. The wings are next. The balls of my feet move to the side, brush the floor, then come back in. My arms circle to the sides like propellers.

"Looking great!" Ms Anne calls above my tapping.

I grin and move easily into the heel stand. *One, two, three, four, five. Now for the end.* I jump on my right foot, then brush the floor with the ball of my left foot. *One, two.* I jump on my left foot and bring my right ankle to the left knee, then repeat the buffalo with my other leg.

I finish with the shuffles. My feet glide on the floor, making the best *click-clack* sound. This is my happy place again. Just me, the music and my feet. No distractions.

"That was some fancy footwork," Ms Anne says when I finish. "I've missed that smile."

I smile wider. "Me too."

I'm so happy that at first I don't even notice the time. But when I look at the clock and see that ballet starts in ten minutes, my stomach drops to the floor.

CHAPTER 9

FINDING MY VOICE

Shaking, I walk slowly into the ballet studio. Brie, Gabby and Jada immediately crowd around me.

Jada squeezes my shoulder. "You'll be fine," she says.

I nod and clutch my water bottle, but I'm too nervous to take a sip. I close my eyes and try to bring back the feeling I had with Ms Anne minutes ago. My feet and I felt at home again.

Ella appears in the doorway in a sparkly, black leotard. "Are you going to finish the class this time?" She smirks at me.

Jada steps in front of me. "Do you have a problem?" she asks.

Ella doesn't flinch. "Not with you."

"That's what you think," says Gabby. "We're all friends here."

Ella shrugs. "*Draaama*," she says before walking to the barre.

"I didn't mean to drag you guys into this," I say quietly.

Jada puts her arm around me. "Don't be silly. You didn't drag us into this. We're your friends. And she doesn't need to make trouble."

"Did you tell Ms Anne? What did she say?" asks Brie.

"And your mum?" asks Gabby.

"She only does it when no one is watching, and I . . . didn't tell them." I lace my fingers together. "I've been hoping to deal with it on my own. I don't want to worry my mum."

"I understand," says Gabby. "But if she keeps bullying you, we should say something."

"We're here for you," says Brie.

I give her a hug as Ms Marianne walks in. Then we all walk to the barre.

Ella moves over so she's near me. She waits until Ms Marianne turns on the music before hissing in my ear, "Isn't it time for another leotard? I bet the charity shop has more."

I try to move away and practise my *pliés*. But Ella won't let it go. "*Soooo* sorry," she whispers, poking me in the side.

I look at Gabby, Brie and Jada. Anger flashes in their eyes. I clench my fists. Ella doesn't get to ruin this dance school for me. My mum worked too hard to get me here.

Moving even closer, Ella pushes me, and I stumble. "Must be the second-hand shoes," she says louder.

Tears push at my eyes, but they aren't going to stop me this time. I turn so fast, Ella loses her balance. "Enough," I say.

She's facing me now, nostrils flaring. "Are you saying those shoes aren't second-hand?"

I take a deep breath. "So what if they are? They don't stop me from dancing. Neither does this leotard. The only thing stopping me is *you*." I don't realize I'm raising my voice until I notice girls gathering around us. "You," I say again, "are. Always. In. My. Face. I'm here to dance. What are *you* here to do?"

Ella flounders. She looks at the group.

Ms Marianne walks in our direction. "What's going on here?"

Ella is silent, but this time I'm not. "Ella won't leave me alone," I say. "She keeps making rude comments about my shoes and my dance clothes. And she just pushed me."

Now Ms Marianne looks angry. "Is that true?" she asks, looking at us.

My friends nod. So do some of the other dancers who had seen what happened. Ella glares at me, still not saying anything.

"This dance school is about respect, Ella," Ms Marianne says. "Not about who's wearing what. If you can't respect that, I'm not sure this is the right school for you."

Ella snorts. "Whatever. I don't need this place!" she snaps. "I'm too good for this school anyway." She grabs her water and marches out of the studio.

I stare after her open-mouthed. "What just happened?" I whisper.

"You got your voice back," says Jada.

Ms Marianne puts her hand on my shoulder. "How long has Ella been treating you this way?" she asks.

I shift my feet uncomfortably. "Always."

"I'm so sorry I didn't realize what was happening sooner. I never want my students to feel like you must have." Ms Marianne hugs me.

"Thank you," I say.

"You were fabulous," says Gabby.

"It helped knowing you are all here for me," I say.

Ms Marianne turns on the music, and we all go back to the barre. I let the music fill me. I know I'll have to see Ella at school tomorrow, but I'm not scared anymore. I stood up to her once. I can do it again.

CHAPTER 10

NEW FRIENDS

On Thursday, I don't linger at my locker before going into lessons. I'm not going to put up with Ella's bullying anymore.

Here goes nothing, I think as I slide into my seat in Ms DiSousa's classroom.

I don't have to spend much time wondering what's going to happen. Ella is by my desk almost immediately. Ms DiSousa is still standing by the door and not looking in our direction.

"I'm so glad I'm finished with your rubbish dance school," sneers Ella.

"Me too," I say.

Ella frowns and turns her attention to my clothes. She pulls on my yellow jumper. "When are you going to get clothes that fit?"

My face turns red. *Don't let her get to you.* "I like my clothes."

She laughs. "Someone has to."

In front of me, Maddie spins around in her seat. Her bracelet charm jingles. "*I* like that jumper," she says, smiling. "Yellow looks really good on you."

I study her smile. It looks real and not like she's teasing me. "Thank you."

"Seriously?" Ella asks. "You know she got it at a charity shop or something, don't you?"

Maddie stands up. Her head only reaches Ella's ear, but that doesn't seem to bother her.

"Who cares?" She turns her back on Ella and faces me. "Have you ever been to Sunny's Second-hand Shop? I love that place."

My heart beats quickly. I look around the room as I realize something – I judged these girls based on what they were wearing. That's exactly what Ella did to me. But that ends now.

"I love that place too," I say.

"What are you guys talking about?" Olivia asks, glancing over at us.

"Sunny's," says Maddie. "Have you ever been there?"

Olivia shakes her head. "What is it?"

I take a deep breath and say, "It's a second-hand shop. It sells previously worn clothing, but the stuff is all really cool and in great condition."

"Sounds good," says Olivia, nodding. "Maybe I'll go and have a look."

Ella grits her teeth. Before she can say anything else, the bell rings and Ms DiSousa walks into the room.

"Right, where were we last lesson?" she asks as she sits down at her desk.

Ella stomps to her seat, and Maddie sits back down in front of me. But then she turns around and taps her nails on her desk to get my attention. "Let's go to Sunny's this week," she whispers as Ms DiSousa turns to the white board.

"Awesome!" I say.

Ella mumbles something behind me, but that's all she says for the rest of the lesson. She doesn't kick my chair or poke me. When the bell rings to end the day, she grabs her books and rushes out.

I hug my books to my chest and walk to my locker. I see the kids in the corridor in a new way. No one is staring at me or paying attention to what I'm wearing. Perhaps they never did.

I grab my coat and backpack, adjust my headband and step outside. The sun is shining, and I soak it in.

Tomorrow, Ms Marianne's will be my happy place again. What's even better is that school won't be a place I dread anymore. No more clammy hands, no more stomach tied in knots, no more feeling bad about myself.

"See you later!" Maddie and Olivia call as they rush past me.

Days ago, I wouldn't have wanted to draw attention to myself. I would have wondered what they really thought of me.

Today, I shout back, "See you later!"

I've finally found my voice, and I don't want to hold back anymore.

ABOUT THE AUTHOR

Margaret Gurevich is the author of many books for children, including *Gina's Balance*, *Aerials and Envy*, and the award-winning Chloe by Design series. She has also written for *National Geographic Kids* and Penguin Young Readers. While Margaret hasn't done performance dance since she was a tween, this series has inspired her to take dance classes again. She lives in New York, USA, with her son and husband.

ABOUT THE ILLUSTRATOR

Claire Almon lives and works in Georgia, USA, and holds a BFA in illustration from Ringling College of Art and Design, as well as an MFA in animation from Savannah College of Art and Design. She has worked for clients such as American Greetings, Netflix and Cartoon Network and has taught character design at Savannah College of Art and Design. She specializes in creating fun, dynamic characters and works in a variety of mediums, including watercolours, pen and ink, pastel and digital.

GLOSSARY

abuela grandmother

barre horizontal wooden bar used by dancers for support and balance

choreographer person who creates a sequence of steps for a dance routine

combination in dance, a mixture or sequence of two or more patterns of movements or steps

dread fear greatly

loom appear in a large, strange or frightening form, often in a sudden way

routine part (of a performance) that is carefully worked out so it can be repeated often

second-hand shop shop that buys or sells items that have already been owned or used, usually at a less-expensive price

sincere trustworthy and genuine

upstage steal attention away from

TALK ABOUT IT!

1. Why do you think Ella was so focused on bullying Grace, both at school and at Ms Marianne's? Talk about some possible reasons.

2. Do you think Grace should have told her mum or one of her teachers what was going on? How would you have handled the situation?

3. Bullying can be more than just unpleasant – it can be dangerous. Talk about some ways to combat bullying if you see it happening.

WRITE ABOUT IT!

1. Grace realizes that she judged the other girls at her school, just like Ella did to her. Write about a time you judged someone before getting to know them. How did that person end up being different from the way you imagined?

2. Brie, Jada and Gabby all stand up for Grace. Write about a time a friend stood up for you or a time you stood up for a friend. How did it help or change the situation?

3. Ms Marianne's Academy of Dance is Grace's happy place. Do you have a place that makes you feel safe and at home? Write about it! Explain what the place is and why it makes you feel happy.

TAP DANCE STARS

Here are some famous dancers from stage and screen who left their unique marks on the tap world!

Fred Astaire brought his signature tap style to big Hollywood films of the 1930s–1950s. Acting talent and incredible fancy footwork made Astaire an instant star; his work was the product of constant practice, though he made dancing look effortless. His tap routines are still cherished by the dance world. Astaire's career lasted many years, and he was awarded the American Film Institute's Lifetime Achievement Award in 1981.

Eleanor Powell was an American actress and dancer. She had a very athletic and powerful style of dancing. Powell made 14 films during the 1930s and 1940s. She was best known for performing solo tap dances in films such as *Born to Dance*, *Broadway Melody of 1936* and *Lady Be Good*. In 1965, an organization called Dance Masters of America named Powell the World's Greatest Tap Dancer.

Ginger Rogers was Fred Astaire's partner in films and on stage. She was a dancer and an actress and shone as a talent alongside Astaire, as well as in her own right. In 1940, Rogers won an Oscar for Best Actress in a Leading Role for her performance in *Kitty Foyle*. As a duo, Rogers and Astraire did wonders for the popularity of tap dancing and musicals around the world.

Gene Kelly was another dancer who made the films of the 1940s and 1950s come to life with his unique tap routines. Kelly was also the choreographer and producer for some of the films he starred in. His most iconic scene is his rain-splashing dance from *Singin' in the Rain*, known to many as one of the best musicals ever made.

Gregory Hines was a celebrated tap dancer, musician, actor and director. He studied dance from a young age and began a successful Broadway career in the 1970s. He later starred in numerous films and became a household name. In 1992, Hines won a Tony Award for Best Actor in a Musical.

THE FUN DOESN'T STOP HERE!

DISCOVER MORE AT
WWW.RAINTREE.CO.UK